B55 074 914 7

KU-407-190

Rotherham Libraries

B55 074 914 7

PETERS	25-Jan-2022
	12.99
CHILD	RTWTH

For Moranne

First published 2021 by Walker Books Ltd
87 Vauxhall Walk, London SE11 5HJ

2 4 6 8 10 9 7 5 3

© 2021 Jon Klassen

The right of Jon Klassen to be identified as the
author and illustrator of this work has been asserted by him
in accordance with the Copyright, Designs and Patents Act 1988

This book has been typeset in Helvetica

Printed in China

All rights reserved. No part of this book may be reproduced, transmitted or stored
in an information retrieval system in any form or by any means,
graphic, electronic or mechanical, including photocopying, taping and
recording, without prior written permission from the publisher.

British Library Cataloguing in Publication Data:
a catalogue record for this book is available from the British Library

ISBN 978-1-4063-9557-0

www.walker.co.uk

THE
ROCK
FROM
THE
SKY

Jon Klassen

WALKER BOOKS
AND SUBSIDIARIES

LONDON · BOSTON · SYDNEY · AUCKLAND

1.

THE

ROCK

I like standing in this spot. It is my favourite spot to stand.

I don't ever want to stand anywhere else.

Hello.

Hello. What are you doing?

I am standing in my favourite spot. Come. Stand in it with me.

OK.

What do you think
of my spot?

Actually I have a
bad feeling about it.

A bad feeling?

Yes.

There is another spot
over there. Do you see it?

Yes. I see it.

I will go and stand in it,
to see if it feels better
than this spot.

HOW DOES THAT SPOT FEEL?

I CANNOT HEAR YOU.
YOU ARE TOO FAR AWAY.
I AM GOING TO COME BACK.

Does this spot still feel bad?

Yes. It feels even worse than before. I am going back to the other spot. Do you want to come with me?

No. I will stay here.
This is my favourite spot.

Are you sure?

Yes.

Oh, hello.
I am standing in
this spot by myself.
Come. Stand in it
with me.

MY SPOT IS BETTER.

YOU ARE TOO FAR AWAY TO HEAR.

I AM COMING CLOSER.

WE STILL CANNOT HEAR YOU.

I said my spot is better.

2.

THE

FALL

Hello.

Hello.

What happened?

Nothing.

Were you
climbing
on it?

No.

Did you
fall off?

No.

Do you need help?

No. I do not need help.

OK.

I never need help.

OK.

What are *you* doing?

I came to take a nap.
It is nice under here.
You can take a nap
too, if you want.
There is just enough
room for two.

No. I am not tired.

OK.

I am never tired.

OK.

3.

THE

FUTURE

What are you doing?

I like to close my eyes and imagine into the future.

Are you doing it right now?

Yes. Come. Close your eyes and do it with me.

In the future, this spot will look different.

New things will grow.

New plants and trees will come.

A whole forest maybe.

It is nice here.

Yes. It is.

Wait, what is that?
Does something live here?

Maybe. I don't know.

What is it?

We are in the future.
I don't know what it is.

What is it doing?

SHHH, it will hear you.

AAAAAAAAAAAA!!

SHHHHHHHHH!!

AAAAAAAAAAAA!!

OK, OK, I THINK IT'S GOING.

OK, it's gone.

I don't want to imagine into the future with you anymore.

4.

THE

SUNSET

I like to sit and watch
the sunset. My favourite
part is at the very end.

This is a good spot to
watch it from. There is
nothing in the way.

HELLO.

Hello.

WHAT ARE YOU DOING?

We are watching the sunset.

I DID NOT HEAR YOU. I AM
GOING TO COME CLOSER.

OK. WHAT ARE YOU DOING?

We are watching the sunset.

I STILL CANNOT HEAR YOU.

I AM GOING TO COME CLOSER AGAIN.

OK. What are you doing?

We are not doing it anymore.

5.

NO

MORE

ROOM

I see. I see how it is.
Just enough room for two.

Maybe I will go to the other spot by myself.

Maybe I will never come back.

I SAID MAYBE I WILL NEVER
COME BACK.

Maybe I am too far away for
them to hear.

I will go back closer and tell them again.

I said maybe I will never come back.